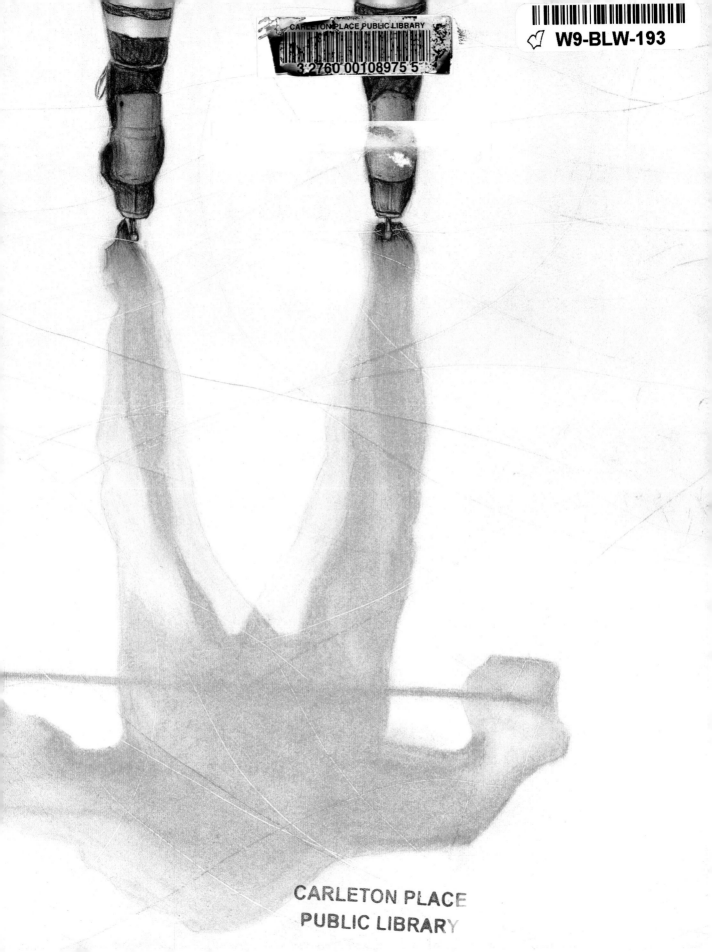

W9-BLW-193

With an afterword by
BOBBY ORR

THE BOY IN NUMBER FOUR

By **KARA KOOTSTRA**

Illustrated by **REGAN THOMSON**

In the ice rink locker room sat
the boy in Number Four,
lacing up his skates like so
many times before.

He thought of all his practices,
some early and some late.

The drills that he would
do to help him...

pass   and shoot

and skate.

There were times when it was easy,
and others that were tough,
but even when it seemed too hard,
he never would give up.

He'd sometimes get an injury,
a broken bone or bruise,

and though they did try hard to win,
sometimes his team would lose.

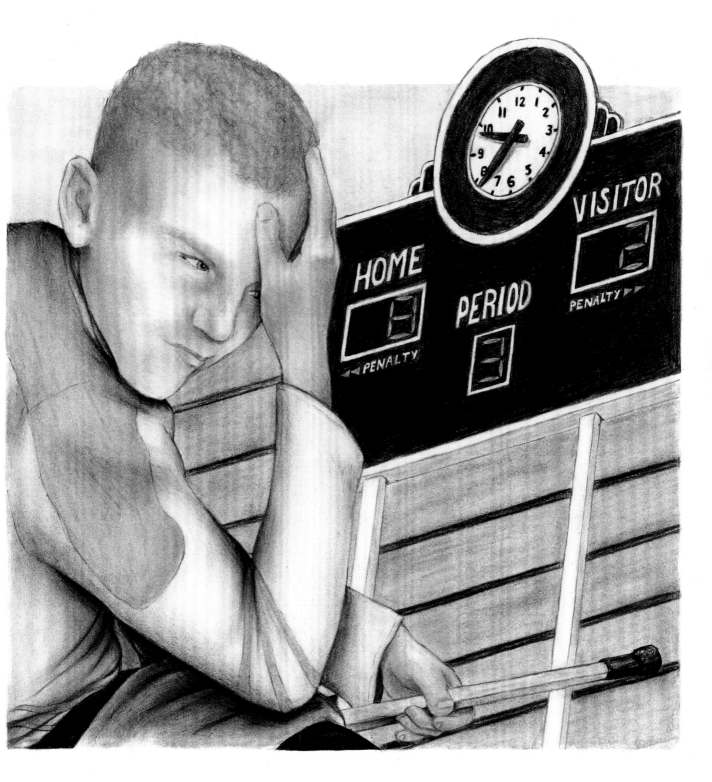

But the boy in Number Four
had a passion and a dream...
to one day be a player on a
big league hockey team!

Passing, shooting, skating, his coaches led the way,

and taught him to respect
both teams when it
was time to play.

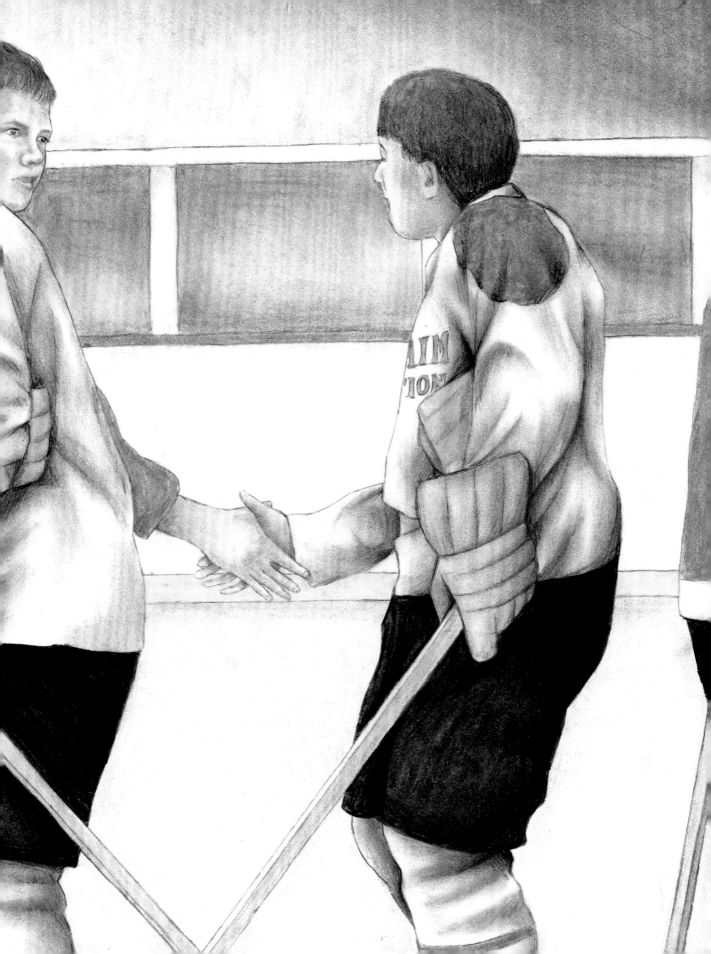

For months and months
he'd practised.
Now the game was
due to start...

he skated out
before the crowd,
excitement in
his heart.

The whistle blows, the puck is dropped,
and off speeds Number Four,

passing

shooting

skating

like so many
times before.

He sweeps around behind the net and
up the ice he races, his skate blades flash
from left to right in front of cheering faces.

Another player passes–now the puck is Number Four's.

His eyes can see the net in front. He steadies, shoots...

he scores!

It's a goal for Number Four!
A game-winning goal for the amazing

Bobby Orr!

Afterword by
BOBBY ORR

When I was growing up, hockey was a very important part of my world. During the winter months my friends and I would play anywhere we could find ice — on Georgian Bay or the Seguin River or at a schoolyard rink. It really didn't matter where. As long as we could play hockey we were happy. I'd leave in the morning with my hockey stick and skates slung over my shoulder, and often my parents would say no more than "be home by dark." Sometimes we kept score, sometimes we didn't, but mostly our games were about the sheer joy of play, of being able to go outside with your buddies and simply have a good time. In those days, we didn't wait for an adult to organize our social time or sports experiences. We took that upon ourselves. We were the ones who decided when to get together, which game to play, and who would be on whose team. I'm a firm believer in kids just getting out and playing any kind of sport. Being part of a team, official or otherwise, should not just be an experience for the elite player. It should be something every child has a chance to experience.

The illustrations in this book are based in large part on photos of me, growing up playing hockey. I learned a lot during all those years, honing the techniques and skills that would allow me to play against grown men while I was still a young teen. But most importantly, I learned respect — for the game itself and for everyone involved in it: my parents, who supported me throughout my childhood and career, my teammates and coaches, and members of opposing teams as well.

Today, thousands of kids growing up all around the world may be dreaming about making it to the NHL, and some may even succeed. But for everyone who loves hockey — young or old, player or spectator — I hope this book inspires you to simply pick up a stick, get together with some friends, and just have some fun playing the best game on earth.

To my father, Vern, the coach; my husband, Kyle, my teammate;
and to Nate and Claire, my biggest fans.

~ KK ~

To my husband, Steve, and my five children,
who are the best support team and inspiration that this mom could ask for.

~ RT ~

PUFFIN

an imprint of Penguin Canada Books Inc., a Penguin Random House Company

Published by the Penguin Group

Penguin Canada Books Inc., 90 Eglinton Avenue East, Suite 700, Toronto, Ontario, Canada
M4P 2Y3

Penguin Group (USA) LLC, 375 Hudson Street, New York, New York 10014, U.S.A.
Penguin Books Ltd, 80 Strand, London WC2R 0RL, England
Penguin Ireland, 25 St Stephen's Green, Dublin 2, Ireland (a division of Penguin Books Ltd)
Penguin Group (Australia), 707 Collins Street, Melbourne, Victoria 3008, Australia (a division of Pearson Australia Group Pty Ltd)
Penguin Books India Pvt Ltd, 11 Community Centre, Panchsheel Park, New Delhi – 110 017, India
Penguin Group (NZ), 67 Apollo Drive, Rosedale, Auckland 0632, New Zealand (a division of Pearson New Zealand Ltd)
Penguin Books (South Africa) (Pty) Ltd, 24 Sturdee Avenue, Rosebank, Johannesburg 2196, South Africa

Penguin Books Ltd, Registered Offices: 80 Strand, London WC2R 0RL, England

First published 2014

1 2 3 4 5 6 7 8 9 10

Manufactured in China.

LIBRARY AND ARCHIVES CANADA CATALOGUING IN PUBLICATION

Kootstra, Kara, 1982-, author
The boy in number four / Kara Kootstra ; illustrated by Regan Thomson ;
afterword by Bobby Orr.

For ages 4 and up.
ISBN 978-0-670-06713-8 (bound)

1. Orr, Bobby, 1948- --Juvenile literature. 2. Hockey players--Canada--Biography--Juvenile literature.
3. Hockey--Juvenile literature. I. Thomson, Regan, 1981-, illustrator II. Title.

GV848.5.O7K65 2014   j796.962092   C2014-902775-3

Visit the Penguin Canada website at www.penguin.ca

Special and corporate bulk purchase rates available; please see www.penguin.ca/corporatesales or call 1-800-810-3104, ext. 2477.